PRAISE FOR M. L. BUCHMAN

Top 10 Romance of 2012, 2015, and 2016.

— BOOKLIST: THE NIGHT IS MINE, HOT
POINT, HEART STRIKE

One of our favorite authors.

— RT BOOK REVIEWS

Buchman has catapulted his way to the top tier of
my favorite authors.

— FRESH FICTION

A favorite author of mine. I'll read anything that
carries his name, no questions asked. Meet your
new favorite author!

— THE SASSY BOOKSTER, FLASH OF
FIRE

M.L. Buchman is guaranteed to get me lost in a
good story.

— THE READING CAFE, WAY OF THE
WARRIOR: NSDQ

I love Buchman's writing. His vivid descriptions
bring everything to life in an unforgettable way.

— PURE JONEL, HOT POINT

THEY BOTH HOLD THE TRUTH

AN OREGON FIREBIRDS ROMANCE

M. L. BUCHMAN

Buchman Bookworks

Other works by M. L. Buchman:

<u>The Night Stalkers</u>
MAIN FLIGHT
The Night Is Mine
I Own the Dawn
Wait Until Dark
Take Over at Midnight
Light Up the Night
Bring On the Dusk
By Break of Day
WHITE HOUSE HOLIDAY
Daniel's Christmas
Frank's Independence Day
Peter's Christmas
Zachary's Christmas
Roy's Independence Day
Damien's Christmas
AND THE NAVY
Christmas at Steel Beach
Christmas at Peleliu Cove
5E
Target of the Heart
Target Lock on Love
Target of Mine

<u>Firehawks</u>
MAIN FLIGHT
Pure Heat
Full Blaze
Hot Point
Flash of Fire
Wild Fire
SMOKEJUMPERS
Wildfire at Dawn
Wildfire at Larch Creek
Wildfire on the Skagit

<u>Delta Force</u>
Target Engaged
Heart Strike
Wild Justice

<u>Where Dreams</u>
Where Dreams are Born
Where Dreams Reside
Where Dreams Are of Christmas
Where Dreams Unfold
Where Dreams Are Written

<u>Eagle Cove</u>
Return to Eagle Cove
Recipe for Eagle Cove
Longing for Eagle Cove
Keepsake for Eagle Cove

<u>Henderson's Ranch</u>
Nathan's Big Sky

<u>Love Abroad</u>
Heart of the Cotswolds: England

<u>Dead Chef Thrillers</u>
Swap Out!
One Chef!
Two Chef!

<u>Deities Anonymous</u>
Cookbook from Hell: Reheated
Saviors 101

<u>SF/F Titles</u>
The Nara Reaction
Monk's Maze
the Me and Elsie Chronicles

<u>Strategies for Success (NF)</u>
Managing Your Inner Artist/Writer
Estate Planning for Authors

1

$\mathcal{T}$y had trouble keeping his attention on the road. The steeply-jagged peaks of the Selway-Bitterroot Wilderness towered close over either side of Montana's Highway 93 and he kept hunching over the wheel to crane upward. He'd traveled this road a hundred times growing up, but a summer of working for the Oregon Firebirds had given him a whole new calibration for how rugged it was.

As he raced along—the third pickup in a line of three —Ty Franks decided that it had been a near perfect summer in ways he'd never expected. And definitely nothing like he'd planned.

Getting hired by the Firebirds as a Ty-of-all-trades handyman had always been his plan. He had to find out all he could about the owners Curt and Jana Williams— brother and sister. But he'd had fun with the team which was a complete and unexpected bonus. A bonus that was fast becoming a burden.

Despite being just a summer hire, the Firebirds team had tried to make him one of their own. They'd certainly welcomed him as if he had always been. And, now that the summer was ending and the northern fire season was drawing to a close, he wished that he'd let them.

Instead, he'd done his best to keep his distance. A distance that was about to grow. The team headed south to fight the inevitable Southern California fires. And he was headed back to school (at least until the University of Montana in Missoula found out he was broke and that he didn't really care about any of their coursework anyway).

Over the last four months he'd willingly helped Jana with operations paperwork and team logistics.

Maggie had taught him the basics of maintaining the helicopters from refueling to checking air filters. By the end of the summer, she trusted him with hydraulics, greasing joints, and a dozen other tasks—both messy and not. She always doublechecked him, because that's the kind of mechanic she was, but she didn't let the pilots do a tenth of the things she'd taught him. When she'd torn apart each of the turbine engines as part of a duty-cycle service, she'd let him be her assistant—like his mom being an OR nurse before she died. He'd handed Maggie tools and parts and asked a thousand questions—that she'd always answered in that cheerful way she had. It had been awesome.

He'd never done long-haul trucking, but he'd grown a taste for it as one of the Firebirds' drivers. The team had three big Denali pickups, each rigged to tow a low-boy trailer with a pair of MD 520N firefighting helicopters strapped on. Within a day, they'd been able to place all six of the helos almost anywhere in the West. They'd fought fires from San Francisco to the Canadian border, from the Oregon Coast over to Idaho.

Right now, by some random chance, they were heading home. He'd grown up in Missoula, Montana, and attended—had attended—university there. His past lay less than an hour ahead, yet it felt like the most foreign place ever. He had no Mom, she'd told him Dad had died in a car wreck when Ty was two, and soon no school. His worldly belongings were in a pack in the back of the truck.

Seeking any distraction, he looked up again at the cloud of smoke. The dirty snarl of ash, bigger than any thunderhead, reached all the way up to the jet stream where it was a sheared-off flattop. Three months ago he'd have thought nothing of it, just some distant storm cloud. Now he knew that was true, but it was a *fire* storm cloud made of smoke. And by the size and color of the column it was big and burning incredibly hot to lift dark ash that high.

He considered waking up Drew and Amos to point it out, but they'd be getting little enough sleep in the next few days as pilots. The other pilots were probably passed out in their own trucks as he, Maggie, and Jana raced them and their helos toward the fire.

It had been funny watching the crew pair off through the summer—and not just for some quick sex. They were engaged, talking weddings. It was weird. Also strange: it hadn't changed who rode with who. Curt, the team's leader, always rode with his sister, Jana. Another pilot Palo always rode with them. And that was despite Curt marrying Stacy and the impending weddings of Palo to Maggie, and Jana to Jasper. It was hard not to envy them. Sure, the women were all much older than he was—late twenties, even thirties—but they were some seriously hot women.

All the couples had been scattered across the trucks for the long drives at the start of the summer. They'd decided to stay that way even after they got together. Maybe they thought it made for happy marriages or some other equally dumb fantasy. Going through his mom's stuff, he'd learned that was all a lie.

"Leaves just us three single guys to whine together," Ty mouthed one of Drew's favorite complaints on his sleeping friend's behalf.

Friends, that was another thing he'd never expected to find among the Oregon Firebirds, but he had. It was easy to see himself hanging with Drew and Amos…except he was almost done with the Firebirds. He'd even toyed with the idea of changing his major from law to forestry, because law was sure as hell a yawner. It was pointless as he'd have to drop out anyway, just like he had last year when Mom got so sick, but—*Shit!*

That got his determination back on track. The Firebirds might think they were nearly done with him, but he was a long way from being done with them. Ty gripped the steering wheel until his knuckles went white and it became hard to steer along the winding two lane. Their parents might be dead too, but the brother and sister had yet to answer for their father.

But if Ty had let himself, sure he could have had fun. Gone to the bar with them, because he had the fake ID to match his summer alias.

Nope! It hadn't matched his plans.

But he was surprised to discover that he wished he had gone anyway.

---

*M*allory Kerr dangled in the trees and debated between screaming and cursing. She had to choose soon, because otherwise she'd start crying—which wasn't ever on her agenda. Not even when her wrist hurt like…well, wildfire.

"What are you doing up there?"

"Enjoying the view," she snapped back over the radio. She finally spotted Krista standing in the dry-grass clearing wearing full smokejumper gear, wrestling her chute into a stuff sack. As she watched, the second stick of jump buddies—Evan and Akbar—floated into the clearing as if it was the easiest thing in the world.

"Okay, let me rephrase. Why aren't you doing anything about it?" The tiny Krista far below didn't even turn to look up—she just knew.

"The view is pretty," Mallory told her partner, even if she hadn't looked around at it yet. Humor, there was a path away from screaming, cursing, *or* crying and she took it. "And I screwed up my wrist."

The tiny figure far below stopped with all the chute packing then shaded her eyes to really look up at Mallory. When she pulled out her binoculars, Mallory started feeling less comfortable—like a squirrel in a tree.

"Huh!" Krista's grunt didn't make her feel much better.

Looking away, Mallory did finally see the view, which was stunning—one of the things she loved about smokejumping. She'd always liked the outdoors, but now she lived in it—had a job saving it.

The sharp mountain slopes of the Selway-Bitterroot Wilderness soared around her. Douglas fir stood proudly above tangled ranks of scrub alder and stone outcroppings. The clearing she'd been aiming for had been so close, but the capricious fire-driven wind had backed at the wrong moment and stolen most of her lift. She dropped vertically faster than any elevator, even flying briefly backwards. That's when she'd been slammed into this tree and snagged her chute.

Keeping her injured hand tight against her chest, she swung out a leg and then kicked it around like a ballet spin. Despite the harness she dangled from facing her outwards, she was able to twist enough to see what she'd landed in.

"Oh crap!" Mallory now saw what had earned her Krista's grunt. She'd managed to catch her parachute on an old king of the forest—on its very thinnest and uppermost branches.

Then she made the mistake of looking straight down as the harness spun her to face away from the tree once more. Heights never bothered her, at least not while the parachute was flying, but she was a long way up, on a very dead tree. Each breath she took might have enough force to snap the tip in two and dash her down to the forest floor.

Because of how she'd snagged, she was about ten feet out into space from the trunk.

She didn't dare try pumping herself back and forth like a swing to reach the trunk. The slim treetop didn't even have a handy branch to grab and pull herself in. There was also no question of anyone climbing the tree to get to her—not unless they both wanted to die.

Looking down once more, she saw Krista hauling climbing gear out of her bag, even as the other smokies stopped her. It was suicide to climb up, but it took both of them to argue Krista out of trying anyway. Mallory knew she'd do the same—she'd do anything for Krista.

They'd met three years ago at a three-day smokejumpers adventure camp Krista had organized for high school girls. It had changed the direction of her life—as in she finally had one. In the two years she'd been jumping with Krista and the Mount Hood Aviation smokies, she'd only snagged one other tree—one of the best jump records in the entire team. That one she'd been able to climb down from without even needing a line. This one was going to suck.

"Can you at least get a line around the trunk?" Krista asked after the others had finally stopped her efforts.

Mallory had a hundred feet of 9mm climbing line coiled in the calf pouch of her Kevlar jumpsuit, on the same side as her bunged up wrist. She managed to snag one end of it with an awkward mid-air kneel and cross-reach. And there she hung, stupidly holding one end of the line in her only good hand, completely unable to see the trunk. Normally, she could tie on a small grapple, toss it over a branch, and pull herself in. But in her mind's eye she could still see the smooth, branchless expanse of this section of trunk. Nothing to hook onto.

Not good!

Again the need to scream surged into her hard enough to force a few tears from her eyes when she wouldn't give it a voice.

Be calm. Be rational. She went back over her training.

The only other real option was a direct lowering, tying off to the upper parachute harness, then releasing from it and descending. A hundred feet of line wouldn't get her out of a two hundred-foot tree—especially not one-handed.

"Just wait a moment," Krista thankfully called over the radio before Mallory could reconsider the screaming-cursing-crying emotional triangle.

Not willing to risk another twist, Mallory looked as far as she could north and south—she had a clear view of west. No sign of the fire, which meant it was directly behind her. That got her thinking about the heat-fuel-oxygen *fire* triangle. It was a baking hot summer with a fire coming over the ridge.

They'd jumped well ahead of it, enough to have time to prepare a fire break. But was it far enough? Other than Krista, the ground team—which had been augmented by more sticks of jumpers—were in full-hustle mode. But there was no way to gauge anything from that—smokies *lived* in full-hustle mode. Another thing she'd liked about jumping fires.

The air in the Selway-Bitterroot Wilderness was so fresh (except for the increasing smoke) that it might as well be pure oxygen. And fuel—she was perched two hundred feet up a tree so dead that it had shed its bark, leaving behind a weathered gray patina. About the best fuel there was and it would burn incredibly hot. The moisture in her body wouldn't be much more than a puff of steam if the tree caught fire while she was still in it.

"Help is coming," Krista called. "Just hang in there."

"Oh, like I have a choice." Mallory—or at least her imagination—could already feel the heat at her back.

he line of pickups suddenly jinked over to the side of the road and parked on the gravel shoulder. Ty kept his in the line, even though he didn't know what was going on. They were still thirty miles from Missoula. He nudged Drew and Amos awake.

"Something's up."

They blinked at him uncertainly.

"Ty, you're with me," Stacy grabbed his arm the second he stepped down from the truck and dragged him over to her helo. "Put this on."

Ty held the Nomex fire shirt and pants she'd thrown at him for a long moment. He'd gotten to go aloft on small flights with Maggie when she was testing the results of some of her maintenance work. He'd loved that. Helicopters were so cool. He'd never gotten to take a real flight and definitely not to anywhere he'd need protective gear.

But at the pace everyone was suddenly moving, there was no time to waste. He stripped and changed right there on the shoulder of Highway 93. He kept his head down so that no one could see his embarrassment at standing on a state highway wearing only briefs and a vintage Maroon 5 t-shirt that his mom had gotten years ago. He'd needed the added strength to face returning to the dead end of Missoula. Of course, right now, everything in his life was a dead end, which sucked beyond the depths of suckitude.

Stay focused. Get dressed instead of standing half-naked in the middle of the highway.

It normally took three people fifteen minutes to unload a helo from the lowboy trailer, unfold its rotors, and prepare it for flight. Within seconds, the entire team was grouped around Stacy's helo.

Drew and Amos were sent out in either direction to stop traffic. Everyone else got the machine unloaded onto the highway and fully prepped in under five minutes while people climbed out of their cars to gawk.

Stacy pointed at a headset and shoved him toward the backseat, which didn't seem much fun. The backseat of a firefighting MD 520N wasn't set up for comfort. It didn't even *have* seats—making the backseat phrase kinda pointless. Two seats equaled another five gallons of water-carrying capacity, so they'd been removed to save weight. And now they'd popped off the rear door leaving the rear area exposed to the world. In one corner of the back was a strapped down pile of fire gear: an emergency pack, a Pulaski fire axe, and some other things that he decided he'd rather not know the purpose of.

But, as everyone was in such a rush, he went where he was told. He barely had his safety line snapped in and headset on before Stacy had them aloft, taking off from the middle of Route 93. Before they disappeared out of sight below, he could see everyone else getting back in the trucks to continue toward Missoula.

There was an audience of over fifty cars watching them. He was down with that.

"Ty, we have a smokejumper snagged high in a tree," Stacy told him over the intercom headset. "No one else can get there as fast as we can, so it's up to us to fish them out."

Okay. That was cool enough to make him glad to sit on the cargo floor for his first real flight.

"Mine is the only Firebirds helo with a winch. You've got about six minutes to make sure you know how to work it. I can run it from here, but I'd rather pay attention to not getting us messed up with the fire."

"I've serviced this with Maggie," he let her know. Then went through it again just to be sure. He ran out ten feet of the steel wire, holding onto the snap hook at the end so that it didn't beat against the outside of the racing helo. Maggie would never forgive him if he scratched the paint on one of her precious birds. He reeled it back in.

"All good," he reported.

That was when he looked down. The terrain away from the highway was even rougher, almost brutal. He'd thought that the Siskiyou Mountains around the Firebirds' base in southwest Oregon were rugged. They were prairie lands compared to this.

Sharp peaks jagged upward out of the forest. The lower slopes were thick with trees except where long lines of bare rock showed winter avalanche scrapes. Perched atop one peak, he spotted a tiny lookout tower. He waved back at the couple watching him from the small hut atop the tall stilts.

It seemed like everyone was a couple, except for he, Drew, and Amos all relegated to their bachelor truck. Didn't matter. Not really. Even if it kinda did. He didn't believe in such shit, but they all made it look awfully—

Stacy's curse had him looking forward. Stacy never swore.

Glad that he'd kept his sunglasses, he leaned his face out into the wind through the open doorway. It only took a second to spot the black-and-red-flame parachute. It was snagged in the top of the tallest pine around—way at the top. If they screwed this up, the smokejumper was going to fall over two hundred feet and turn into a small, bloody patch on the rocks below.

Somehow it brought the whole summer into focus. He'd spent his days hanging around camp. Waiting for the helos to come back so that he could help clean them up and cram some calories into the pilots to get them back aloft. As for the fires, he'd only seen them from a distance or on the ground after they were burned out and the team was driving away.

Now they were flying toward an entire mountain sheathed in smoke and flames that reached twice the height of the trees. Even as he watched, a monster Canadair CL-415 water tanker flew in to dump water on the fire. He'd stood beside those at various airports over the summer—they were humungous. But on this fire, it looked like a tiny model plane dumping a Dixie cup of water on the massive conflagration.

"You fly into that?"

"Not unless we have to," Stacy replied. "The Firebirds are specialists in saving structures: homes, barns, businesses. We typically leave the monster wildfires for the big boys whenever we can. Though we've killed a lot of spot fires around the main firefight when we're called into the fray. Get the winch going."

He spooled it down as Stacy slowed and maneuvered above the trapped smokejumper. Ty kept an eye on the drum. Maggie had told him to never run it all the way out, but to always keep a few wraps of the wire on the drum for extra safety. He was the one who'd thought up painting the last ten feet bright red which had earned him a hard hug. It was quick—and she was older and engaged to Palo who could probably beat up Ty with his pinkie—but…damn!

"That's it," he announced as the first of the red spooled out and he stopped the winch. He then rested a hand on the wire to try and damp out the swinging motion.

"Let me bring it to the smokie," Stacy slowed even more. "If you try to swing it to them, we could snag a branch or miss completely."

So he concentrated on just keeping it steady as Stacy maneuvered them in above the smokejumper. He could see a cluster of a dozen more smokies who had now formed up in the clearing below. Even as he watched, they began cutting down the trees. Two fell almost simultaneously— well away from the one with the smokie caught in its branches. Though Ty could see them glancing aloft as they moved to the next trees.

He was on display. Center stage. And whatever anger he felt toward the owners of the Firebirds, he really didn't want to screw up.

---

4

*M*allory watched the approaching helo from one direction. The rapidly thickening smoke from behind. And her jump team shifting into action below.

"Wish I was with you guys." Because if she was, she wouldn't be dangling up here with her wrist swelling painfully against the glove and cuff of her jump gear. She considered easing it, but even the thought of touching it sent shivers through her. Shivers that she hoped the dead tree didn't pick up on and decide it was time to snap off. Besides, if it was a bad break, the cuff might be the only thing stabilizing her wrist.

She could feel the downdraft of the helo's rotor blades wash over her and she just prayed that they didn't drive her out of the tree.

The wire cable flashed by fifty feet from her. That wasn't going to help at all, but she did her best to keep her eyes on it. She considered lifting her wire jump mask to get a better view, but decided to leave it in place so that she didn't get face-lashed by the swinging cable.

The next time it was only twenty feet away when it flashed by going the other way.

Ten and moving slower.

Five.

She lunged for it at three, which was a mistake. Because she was dangling, the lunge caused her body to twist out of the way. Then there was a sickening moment of weightlessness as one of the branches holding her parachute gave way. She dropped five feet before it caught again. A broken branch thudded off her jump helmet before it disappeared below. "So long, pal. Hope I don't see you soon."

Mallory had also lost sight of the cable.

It slapped hard against her bad wrist and she couldn't fight the scream of pain. She instinctively wrapped her good arm over her bad wrist to protect it and by pure luck, pinned the cable against her body.

The hook. How far down was the hook?

She very carefully trapped the cable against her body with her bad arm and began yanking it upward with her good hand. Ten feet. Twenty. At twenty-five she had the hook. Another instant and she had it securely snapped into the big D-ring on the front of her harness. Her heartrate decelerated from blind panic to mere overdrive. Overdrive she could deal with.

Mallory held her arms straight out to either side, ignoring the shooting pain of her unsupported wrist so that they'd know she was clear to lift.

It took forever, but the slack came out of the winch cable. They eased her out and away from the tree. The pressure came off the parachute harness. Then there was a sharp yank where the parachute attached at her shoulders. It flipped her upside down.

She slapped for the main chute cutaway.

Even as she yanked the double cord, dangling feet to the sky, she could see her parachute, snarled in the broken-off top of the tree, plummeting downward.

The triple-ring attachment released and she sprang upward against the helo's pull. Bouncing hard several times before she once more flipped right side up. Her bad hand got pinned between the winch cable and her chest.

She heard the start of her own scream, but thankfully passed out before she could hear the end of it.

"*Y*ou stick with him until his own people arrive." Stacy was landing them gently on the giant green shamrock that marked the rooftop helipad of the St. Patrick Hospital in downtown Missoula. Ty could see a medical team waiting nearby with a gurney.

"Her," he managed to croak out.

"What's that?"

"Never mind. I'll stick."

He'd winched the unconscious smokejumper aloft as Stacy had raced toward the hospital. With no spare room, he'd dragged the smokie into his lap. He'd left the winch cable attached to the smokie's harness and wrapped his arms around both the harness and the jumpsuit for stability during the wild flight around the bucking fire winds.

That's when he'd learned just how much of the person's bulk was jumpsuit and how little of it was smokejumper.

A peek through the wire mesh on the front of the

helmet revealed a pale, slender face, and a long loop of white-blonde hair.

The smokejumper was a she. He took the liberty of swinging up her mask to make sure she was still breathing. Her face wasn't pretty, it was gorgeous. Like model gorgeous. Prettier than any girl guys like him ever got to hold—even when passed out in full smokejumper gear.

He'd nearly choked when their helicopter had briefly been dragged downward by the broken treetop snarled in the jumper's parachute. After she'd released it, he'd only been able to watch in horror as treetop and parachute plummeted into the towering forest below while the smokejumper's body had bounced and flipped at the end of his winch cable like a broken doll.

She was breathing. And beautiful. And young. How could a girl his own age be out doing something as wild as jumping into a wildfire? All he'd done all summer was push papers and polish helicopter windscreens. While she'd been… It was just crazy.

The moment Stacy touched the helo's skids down on the pad, the medical team raced forward, ducking below the spinning rotors. In seconds they had her removed from his lap, on the gurney, and were headed for the elevator.

"Go!" Stacy shouted over the intercom.

Ty lunged forward, and was slammed back into place by his safety line.

Free of that, he was nearly decapitated by the intercom headset, then tangled with the winch hook. He managed to get the former into the pocket on the back of the pilot's seat and snapped the latter onto the keeper loop. He could hear Stacy laughing at him as he sprinted away. He barely cleared the closing doors as he dodged sideways into the elevator.

"You next of kin?" One of the nurses confronted him

as he stumbled for balance, trying not to faceplant atop the smokie still out cold on the gurney.

"Rescue team."

She didn't look impressed.

"I've been ordered to stick with my teammate." The last bit was a bald lie but, like so much of his summer, it was a plausible one.

The nurse finally nodded and turned back to their charge.

Again he was almost left behind when the door on the back side of the elevator was the one that opened.

"What can you tell us?"

"She got her parachute snagged in a treetop."

But what was wrong with her? She'd been conscious when she'd latched herself onto the cable. Then he pictured the painstaking way she'd worked with the cable while he'd held his breath until he could feel himself turning blue.

"Not sure about everything, but there's definitely something with her…" he closed his eyes for a moment to concentrate on the whirl of images, "…left wrist or arm."

They rolled her into an exam room.

One of the attendees probed one arm and then the other. The left one earned the nurse a yelp of pain.

"Ow! Don't touch!"

The smokejumper was suddenly wide awake and staring straight at him with the bluest eyes he'd ever seen.

"Who are you?"

The nurse turned to glare at him.

Crap!

6

*M*allory hadn't been in a hospital except once. Her best friend Meaghan had gotten a bad cut windsurfing out on the Columbia Gorge and needed nine stitches. Mallory had been with her and taken her to…she looked around…maybe this very room. A shocking change from falling out of a tree just a moment before.

She needed one of Meaghan's easy laughs right about now.

Except she was two years gone, off at the University of Washington in Seattle. At seventeen, Mallory had always thought they'd go to the same college, friends for life and all that. Now she was a much wiser twenty and knew that choices could separate people. No one—least of all her parents—understood her sudden change from ballet to smokejumping and forest ecology.

But *she* understood it and that was all that mattered.

"No! It's just my wrist," she protested when they wanted to cut away her Kevlar jumpsuit. It was stupid, but it was her first jumpsuit and it had lasted her for two seasons now. It was just a piece of Kevlar with pockets full of gear, but it was hers—a part of who she was now. No one had believed she could be a smokejumper other than Krista and Evan, her husband. Her parents still didn't. This suit was what had proved them all wrong.

The pain was horrific as they eased open the cuff and got her out of the jumpsuit. Then the Nomex fire shirt that she'd worn over her t-shirt.

To ignore the pain, she kept her attention on the gawky guy still standing at the foot of the bed. He had a thin face and dark eyes, which a sloppy hank of his thick brown hair partially obscured. Kinda broody and intense which she sort of liked.

The nurse was trying to shoo him out and he was edging back under protest. But he wasn't looking at the nurse, he was looking at her like she was some kind of miracle. He wore fire gear and it looked good on him, like it belonged. At the moment she'd gladly take a wildland firefighter over the rather scary doctor and two nurses.

"No, it's okay," she called out.

The nurse huffed out her frustration, but finally departed to other tasks. A bunged-up wrist apparently didn't need two nurses even if chasing off the only even partly familiar thing in the room did.

"Who are you?" Mallory had to focus on something as they prepared her for an x-ray.

"I'm Ba— I'm Ty. Ty Franks," he said it like he was trying to convince himself. "I was up in the helo. I ran the winch."

"Oh. Thanks for that."

He stuck with her through x-ray, doctor consult, a temporary splint, and release. They ended up together on the bench in the front of the hospital, with him hauling her jump gear around over one shoulder. It was a large, awkward mass weighing over fifty pounds—reserve chute plus enough food and gear to work on the fire line for days —but he didn't complain once.

Ty had also done his best to cheer her up as the doctor talked through the steps of recovery. A multiple "simple fracture"—it didn't feel simple. Ice the wrist. Aspirin or ibuprofen. A week in the splint while the swelling subsided, then six weeks in the cast. Done for the fire season. That last had been hard to take, but Ty had told her she was lucky that was all. He'd even made her laugh somehow about a busted wrist being better than becoming a tiny, Mallory-shaped blood splatter on rocks below that old-growth pine.

"Where can I take you?"

She didn't really know. "My jump team will still be in the firefight. Our helos are committed in Reno, Nevada right now. I think our hotshots are at a fire on Washington's Olympic Peninsula. I doubt if our plane pilots stuck around after we jumped."

"You could come hang with us."

"Us?" He hadn't said much except to ask how she was doing every thirty seconds—which was actually kind of sweet because he was so concerned. It had been a while since she'd gobsmacked a seriously cute boy into stuttering silence. Her fellow smokies were all multi-season veterans and much older than she was. The Hoodies—as Mount Hood Aviation's smokejumpers were known—had never taken a rookie, except for her. Mallory had become everyone's little sister on the team. She'd been her school's beauty queen, back when she thought that was important. It was kind of nice having someone see her as female again.

"The Oregon Firebirds. We've got six helos on site. I

figured you'd need a ride, so I called them while you were checking out." Even as he said it, a big black GMC Denali pickup pulled up to the curb. Despite being burdened with her jump gear, he opened and held the front passenger door for her, before clambering in back.

She glanced over at the driver, but her eyes snagged where the woman's hand grabbed the steering wheel. Except it wasn't a hand, it was a pair of steel hooks.

"Hi, I'm Jana."

Mallory looked down at the splint and heavy wrapping around her left wrist. Ty hadn't been kidding. She'd been incredibly lucky. There was no way to be a smokejumper without both hands.

"Hi, I'm Jana," the woman repeated. There was a hint of a laugh as she reached over to lightly tap her hooks against Mallory's splint. The tiniest zing of pain knocked away her surprise.

"Sorry. I, uh—"

"Her name's Mallory," Ty rescued her. "She just found out she's out for the season. I guess it threw her for a loop."

"Kinda," was all she could think to say.

"Be glad that's all it is," Jana briefly flourished her hooks, then used them to drop the truck into gear as if it was the most natural thing in the world.

Six hours ago, everything had seemed so natural in Mallory's world. She was an MHA smokejumper—an elite job in a dangerous profession. She'd even jumped lead stick with Krista—who everyone agreed was absolutely awesome.

Now everything was unnatural, she had nowhere to belong, yet *she* was the lucky one. And she *was*. And even though part of her didn't feel that way, a part of her did.

She knew that was Ty's doing.

Mallory turned around to mouth a 'Thank you' to him. The words caught in her throat. He was staring at her again, like she was a miracle fallen from the sky.

7

Ty knew he wasn't being smooth, but he couldn't seem to do much about it.

Mallory wasn't just beautiful—which she absolutely was—she was also a smokejumper. That was about the coolest thing he could imagine.

He made sure that she was set up in a lawn chair under one of the few shade maples. It was in the grassy area along the edge of their paved corner of the Missoula airport. It was close by the Zulies' white-and-brown headquarters building. The Missoula smokejumpers were fully engaged in this firefight, and all of their tanker assets were as well. There was a hustle and buzz of activity all around them that resounded with activity. Air tankers ripped down out of the sky. In minutes, they were loaded up with a thousand gallons or more of viscous red fire retardant and sent back aloft. It was a bad fire and more assets were streaming in every minute. He recognized outfits from Boise and Utah. No one else from Washington or Oregon yet, but they were facing big fires of their own.

Ty did what he could to make sure Mallory stuck

around as long as possible. Not that there was much he could do, other than make her comfortable. He did place a water bottle close by her good hand after cracking the lid for her. He set a reminder on his phone for two hours so that he could make sure she iced her wrist on schedule and another for three hours when she could take more painkillers.

It was so hard not to stare at her.

Not just the long blonde hair the color of the sun—even nicer than Jana's which was saying something. Or the sky blue eyes. Not even the incredible physique that had been revealed when the nurse had stripped off her Nomex fire shirt and revealed the form-fitting black t-shirt beneath. It was the t-shirt itself that had really gotten him.

This is what AWESOME smokejumpers look like.

Big yellow letters declared it without question. He'd never been that confident about anything in his life. And there Mallory sat, so sure of herself. So perfect.

He jolted to his feet as a flight of the Firebirds came in for service. Amos, Curt, and Jasper on the first flight. Near enough noon. While the trio of helos were refueled and the pilots stretched out the kinks, he scrabbled together food bags for them and cold sodas. They'd already been aloft for four hours while he'd been at the hospital, making this their second refueling stop. Maggie changed air filters without even checking them first. They'd blow them clean and reinsert them on the next service if they were still good. He scrubbed bugs and soot off the windscreens.

In moments they were aloft and the next flight was inbound: Stacy, Palo, and Drew.

"Holy shit!" Drew whispered when he spotted Mallory under the tree.

Ty didn't hesitate. He slammed a water bottle into one of Drew's hands, and then an elbow into his gut.

"Whoa! Sorry man," Drew laughed. "Didn't know you'd already staked the territory."

"I didn't!" How could he? He just didn't like someone else talking about Mallory with that tone. Not even Drew —who he knew was a total dog when it came to women. His and Amos' reputations were notorious on and off the fireline.

"Uh-oh. Somebody's got it bad," Drew's laugh followed him.

He checked in with Palo who didn't offer Mallory more than a glance. "Who's she?"

"She's the smokejumper. Busted-up wrist."

Palo just nodded, then snagged an arm around Maggie's waist as she hurried by. He slammed her into a hug and kiss, then let her go about her work without a single word. But they were both smiling.

Ty couldn't help glancing sideways at Mallory, but she was talking with Stacy.

8

"Thanks for saving me."

"Glad we made it in time. Thanks for being quick to dump your chute when the tree broke. That chunk of tree probably weighed more than my helo. Would have been bad."

Mallory smiled up at Stacy. But she couldn't help notice Ty watching her from under the flop of his hair.

"What's his story?" Then she kinda wished she hadn't asked.

Stacy didn't glance around, but did give her a knowing smile—just the way Meaghan used to when a boy was hitting on Mallory. "Ty has been our handyman all summer. He's good. We're really going to miss him when he goes back to school."

Mallory watched him as he hustled among the three helos. He moved like he knew what he was doing. He also kept doing extra things. Because Stacy wasn't in her helo, Mallory could see him double-checking several things he hadn't on the others and dropping a fresh water bottle into a holder.

"Well, gotta fly now," then Stacy winked at her. "Ty's a damn good kid."

Mallory laughed. Stacy couldn't be more than her late twenties, but they were both "kids" to her. Stacy caught the joke, shrugged good naturedly, and hurried back to her helo. In moments, the three of them were aloft.

Ty spent another twenty minutes dealing with various items—clearly preparing for the next round—then slouched into a chair beside her.

"And now we wait." He didn't sound unhappy about it. Just a fact of life.

"It's weird. I've never seen this part of operations."

"That's because you're always out there being amazing." She wished that he'd tell that to her parents. Her brother would have said it, if he'd come back alive from the Iraq War. He'd have been surprised that she'd broken out of the girly-girl mode she'd been in since forever, but he'd have cheered her on. Two years now and her parents were still waiting for her to "come to her senses."

Ty continued, half speaking to himself. "Thought I was doing something. But you make me feel as if I haven't done shit all summer."

"Stacy seemed to think otherwise. They're all awfully nice."

"I guess," Ty slouched lower.

They chatted through the long afternoon—lazy hours in between moments of frenetic activity. Soon there were the four of them under the tree—Jana with the flight operations radio and Maggie updating her maintenance logs—all shifting their chairs along with the sun to stay in the shade. By late afternoon, it wasn't an issue. The valley where Missoula lay between three mountain ranges slowly filled with smoke until it blocked the sun, erasing shadows. Soon they were donning dust masks.

It took her a while to get comfortable around Jana. That missing hand bothered her more than she wanted to show.

Maggie, who'd just finished another refueling, plummeted into a chair as if exhausted beyond ever moving again.

Mallory had learned through the day that the Firebirds' head mechanic never sat still for long. When she wasn't rushing around a helo, or preparing to, she fussed with the three pickups. No wonder they all looked so perfect. She had a bubbly energy that never let go.

"You two could be sisters," Maggie knocked back half a Coke, as if she needed more caffeine to supercharge her effervescence.

Mallory felt herself turning to face Jana. How close had she come to losing her hand? Then they'd have *really* matched.

"Maybe not sisters, but like really close cousins or something."

Jana, who Mallory had learned didn't speak much, raised her hooks in wry acknowledgement.

Maggie didn't miss the gesture. "Okay. Crappy analogy, but you're both gorgeous blondes. Jana," Maggie leaned forward in a conspiratorial whisper, "swept the feet out from under the ever-so-cute Jasper when she was just ten— even if it took them until last month to figure that out. And now you've knocked our Ty for a total loop. Don't you just love men?" Then she bounced to her feet and was on the move again.

Mallory didn't want to turn to Ty, but couldn't stop herself.

He was frozen as solid as the ice pack he'd fished out of

the cooler and was wrapping in a towel to drape over her arm. He'd been so solicitous all afternoon: remembering when her painkillers were wearing off, making sure she ate and stayed hydrated. He'd even arranged a radio relay though Stacy so that she could check in with Krista and let her jump leader know where she'd ended up—he'd already gotten the message about her wrist relayed while they were still in the hospital.

Through the day, Mallory had come to simply accept Ty's kindness. But Maggie was right, it was more than that. And he wasn't doing the testosterone-poisoned thing either. He was simply taking care of her.

And now he was glowing brighter red than any forest fire.

"Ty?"

"Uh-huh."

"Aren't your hands getting cold?" They were still wrapped around the ice pack.

"Uh-huh." Still he didn't move.

She didn't "just love men" the way Maggie had said it. With her unstoppable effusive energy, and her majorly cute Latina looks, it was easy to bet that men loved her as well.

But Ty was being beyond kind and beyond cute.

Mallory extracted the ice pack from his hands, and laid it over her wrist. After the initial shock, the cold felt good, soothing.

Then she leaned in and brushed her lips over his.

He remained frozen in place, his eyes shooting wide.

Then, just before she was going to pull away, he sighed softly and leaned into the kiss.

9

Ty could feel the shock of the kiss all the way down to his toes. He'd had full-on wild sex that didn't live up to the wonder of Mallory's kiss.

He was supposed to be the worldly one: twenty-one, college-educated (at least partly—not sure why though), and…and…something.

Mallory was just twenty, straight from high school into the smokejumpers, doing her forest ecology coursework mostly online.

Yet he was the one humbled by the fact that she'd kissed him. Humbled and—*Holy Crap, Batman*—majorly turned on. She had a kiss that didn't allow him to do anything but feel and give back the best he could. It was the kind of kiss that didn't allow any chance she was playing a head game—like kissing him at a frat party to upset some boyfriend, or seeking revenge sex, or…

Mallory simply kissed him. And when she was done and moved back, his ears buzzed louder than a flight of incoming helos.

No…exactly that loud.

Jana snapped her hooks together about a half inch off the tip of his nose.

He blinked at her, then at the three helos settling close beside them.

"Yipes!" He pushed out of the chair, but something was wonky with his balance. He shook his head to clear it and got on the move.

Behind him he heard Mallory's delighted laugh, and his equilibrium went haywire again.

10

$\mathcal{B}$ecause she was bored to death, the Firebirds let her help on Day Two. Nothing fancy, handing out water bottles, whatever. Better than sitting still.

Day Three they stopped treating her like some fragile guest and treated her the same way they would anyone else on the team who had a bunged-up wrist.

Krista and the rest of the Hoodies were pulled out on Day Four for a break. The fire was still running ugly, only ten percent contained, but that ten percent had been where the Hoodies had fought it to a standstill. Four days in had earned them twelve hours sack time before they'd be jumping back into a new sector.

Mallory had helped where she could to make sure that the gear was all squared away for the next jump.

"You doing okay, Mal?" Krista was the only one other than her dead brother who got to call her that. Even if becoming a smokie had started as a way to honor his memory, it had now become her lifeblood. They were sitting on the jump deck of a Sherpa C-23 jump plane with their feet dangling just over the airport's tarmac as the sun finished setting. The smoke layer shifted from blood red toward true darkness.

"I am." And she was, much to her own surprise. "I mean I'd rather be jumping but," she raised her arm in its sling and shrugged.

"That's good. You handled that great by the way. Kept your head all the way through. Knew you were something special since that first day."

Mallory bumped shoulders with Krista. Krista was built on a massive scale—at least three Mallorys packed into her powerful frame. She was the big sister Mallory never had and the beloved brother who she'd lost rolled into one.

"Something else on your mind." Krista never missed a thing.

Half a thousand, but Mallory chickened out with the one she already knew the answer to. "Next season?"

"Will take care of next season. You heal up, do whatever the doc says, we'll be jumping together again soon enough."

Mallory planted a kiss on Krista's shoulder. *Best big sister in the world.*

"What's his name?" She didn't miss that either.

"Ty," she sighed. Apparently it was time to jump to the real question.

"Hump him blind yet?"

"Krista!"

"Guess not. Why not?"

"He's just…" she didn't know what. "He's just kind."

"And obviously kisses good enough that you want to hump him blind."

"Krista!"

"Just sayin'. You know how I'm plainspoken and all." And it wasn't an affectation. Her husband and fellow smokie, Evan, often described her as "subtle as an uncontained wildfire"—which was true.

"You never were one to mess around." Krista had never pulled a verbal punch in her life. Probably not a real one either.

"Not once I found Evan."

"And did you hump *him* blind?" Mallory couldn't believe she'd asked the question. Or was even having this conversation.

"Damn straight! About two minutes after your high school's smokejumpers camp with us. You girls left and I dragged him straight off into the woods. We had our way with each other among the ferns. Big time!"

Mallory couldn't help giggling along with Krista's big-throated laugh.

"Gods, I was such a mess at that camp."

"You had it together by the time you left though. Look at yourself, Mal. Look at what you made of yourself. A goddamn smokejumper. Your parents will get that someday, or they won't. Doesn't matter as long as *you* know it. We're tough as Special Forces, Evan always said. He was Green Beret, so I'm gonna trust him on that."

"You just trust him because he married you."

"Yeah," Krista sighed happily. And Krista's bright smile caught the distant airport lights, "He's survived me, too."

"So far," Mallory noted.

"Gives me an idea or two. Wonder if he's still awake." Krista hopped down and patted Mallory's knee before she strode away.

Mallory didn't want to hump Ty blind…except maybe a little. In the evenings, after sunset chased the helicopters from the sky, the Firebirds would all sit around a small firepit, cooking burgers over the flames and telling stories.

Ty had managed to hover and take care of her without making it feel like she was any trouble at all.

She could practically hear Krista's words in Ty's mouth, *A goddamn smokejumper.* She'd impressed the hell out of him. She liked that. A lot. In the past, it had always been her beauty doing the impressing of boys. Ty saw more than that.

After the second night they'd taken a long walk around the airport perimeter, watching the jets from the commercial side of the airport slide in and out through the smoke. Last night, they'd done more than linger along the back fence. They'd done almost everything that could be done while still wearing clothes.

Ty's attraction to her was so big that it seemed to shadow out her past.

When she'd stopped focusing on being the high school's beauty queen, most of her friends had drifted away. As she'd plunged into the academics of botany her senior year, and joined track-and-field to start conditioning her body for the next year's smokejumper tryouts, the boys she used to hang with had drifted away—puzzled by who she'd become. Only her girlfriends in the Outdoors Club, who'd also been at the three-day smokejumpers camp, had understood. Even if they hadn't been prepared for her transformation.

Ty was the first boy who had seen the new her…and couldn't get enough of it.

She could feel him. Out there in the dark even now, waiting for her. Could feel herself wanting to go to him.

11

"*N*ever," was all Ty could manage.

"Never what?" Mallory's voice was barely a breath as she lay beneath him on the blanket. He'd carried it out here, along with a pocketful of foiled-wrapped hope, just on the off chance that she'd come find him and want…

He sighed again, unable to do more. He'd imagined sex with Mallory, but he'd never imagined this.

There was no privacy, no space at the Zulies' base. Especially not with all of the other outfits on site. There were smokies and pilots in every bunk. Hotshots crashed out on the floor and camped on the grass out by the US Forest Service building. Anything as gentle as commercial Boeing 737s roaring along the runway couldn't wake a firefighter fresh off a big burn.

Instead, Mallory had come to him in the place they'd found last night. It was a small wood beyond the north end of the runway, just inside the perimeter fence. Each jet's landing lights flickered through the trees, dappling her perfect body with light flashing faster than a high school gym disco ball. The power of the jets passing less than a hundred feet overhead was nothing compared to the power of what had just passed between them.

When she'd peaked just as a jet had flashed overhead, she'd let loose a laughing scream that overflowed with joy. He'd joined his shout to hers and it had been like nothing before in his life.

"Never what?"

"I'm a guy. I can't speak right now."

"Uh-huh," Mallory kept one arm and both her legs wrapped firmly about him. She snuggled in tighter.

"Never felt anything even close to that. It wasn't just sex. It was… I dunno. Something incredible. You're amazing, Mallory."

"I am. So are you, Ty."

"I wish."

"Hey! How can you not think you're amazing after that? We did really, really good."

Ty hid his face in her hair. Yeah, it was dumb. It was their first time together. But he knew he'd never get tired of Mallory. Not for a minute, not for a second. The smell of her. The taste. The joy that radiated from every move, every look.

It was fine for Ty Franks. He could deserve it. Except he didn't really, because "Ty Franks" didn't exist.

Ty buried his face even deeper in Mallory's glorious hair and wished like hell that he was actually himself and not someone else.

1 2

---

*a*fter ten long days, the fire was drawing to a close. And so was his summer.

None of that mattered anymore.

What mattered was Mallory. They hadn't gone to their wood beneath the jets every night—though each time they did it was even more memorable than the first. But even the nights they'd just lain together in their bags among the sleeping helo pilots curled up on the grass were remarkable.

It was as if the amazing sex was no longer the only thing that mattered. In the past, that had always been the defining and sometimes sole purpose of his relationships. With Mallory it was only one part of an amazing amount of greatness.

She'd unfolded her past like a book. Each page so clear. How the death of her big brother had almost destroyed her until she'd found smokejumping. She understood what parts of herself were broken and had fixed them. She talked about the parts she still didn't understand but was working on. All the time with her head on his shoulder and her injured arm resting negligently on his chest as if they belonged together. As if there was such a thing as being happy together for more than a couple nights.

The passage of time had been marked by little of note. They'd gone back to the hospital for new x-rays and to replace the splint with a cast. The days themselves had been punctuated by good days of hard work. The nights by startling sex and intimate conversation. Or maybe by intimate sex and startling conversation.

He'd told her about his mom, some. Made it clear how much it hurt when she'd died last year so that she'd leave the subject alone. He never mentioned his bastard of a father. Friends growing up. College—leaving after the second week of his junior year to take care of Mom. Those had been safe topics. But he couldn't tell her about anything that really mattered like—

"You're confusing the crap out of me, Mallory." He hadn't really intended to say that to her, but they'd both gotten into the habit of just speaking their thoughts to each other.

"In a good way, I hope," her voice was sleepy and just a little teasing as it often was after what they now called jet-sex.

The wind had shifted three days ago, driving the fire right into the massively prepared firebreaks, and it was dying fast.

It had also flipped the direction of the flight pattern into the airport, because planes always took off and landed into the wind.

Now, instead of idling jets easing down close overhead as if held up by the pillars of their landing lights illuminating columns in the smoke, they roared aloft— heavily laden and under full throttle. The bright landing lights were replaced by little flashes of red and green from the wingtips. And the engines' big-throated howl echoed through their joined bodies as they rode out the jet's passage so close above them. They'd taken to keeping an ear out for jets leaving the terminal and taxiing to the far end of the runway. Getting a good head start on jet-sex had interrupted any number of conversations.

But now when he needed the interruption…

It was late and flights were few and far between.

"Ty?" Mallory murmured into his shoulder.

Her hair lay over his neck and shoulders like a silk blanket. He could lose himself in gliding his hands over the surprising muscles in her sleek frame. From shoulders down to—

"Ty!" She propped herself up with forearm and cast on his chest. The edges of it itched.

"My name isn't Ty."

Mallory jolted as if he'd slapped her.

He lifted his head up to look at her in the soft spill of the airport's lights reflected off the smoky sky. Then, giving up, he thudded the back of his head down on the blanket he'd spread beneath them. He did it again, harder, but it didn't help.

13

----

*M*allory didn't know how to react. A lie? She sworn off those ever since she'd recognized the lie that she was okay with her brother's death. It was only then that she was able to forgive him for dying somewhere so far away. Lies were something high school boys did to get you alone in a dark corner. She knew all about those lies.

But Ty hadn't been like that—except now he said he wasn't Ty. Maybe he was like that. But then why would he confess. He wasn't the only one confused here.

"Who are you?"

"Fuck if I know." He pounded his head back on the ground once more.

"Cut that out!"

He sighed miserably, but stopped.

"Anything else you've been lying about other than your name?" Like how miraculous and important he'd made her feel? Had that been a lie too? She didn't know if she could stand it if it had been.

He tipped his head to one side then the other, before sighing again.

"Not to you. At least not that I can think of."

Mallory sat up, wincing as she forgot to not use her injured hand. She pulled on her shirt, finding it awkward without Ty's help. How many ways had she come to depend on him? But she'd depended on who she *thought* he was. If he was really something else…

"What's your name?"

"Barlow. Barlow Williams."

"I think I like Ty better."

"Barlow Williams the Second. My dad was the First."

She knew who Ty Franks was. Barlow Williams II? Not so much.

"Tyrone was my mom's dad. Franks was her last name."

"So, you *are* Ty, sort of." She knew she was grasping at straws, but she'd come to rely on him far more than made sense. It was as if he was the only one who saw her. Little sister to smokies. "Besieged by some madness," according to her parents' exact words. Ty saw both *her* and the smokejumper. At times it was hard to tell which he was more attracted to and she'd liked that feeling—liked it a lot!

He shrugged a yes then flopped an arm over his eyes.

"Why the lie?" Mallory resisted the urge to just run away.

"God I hate that word. Makes me sound like a total weasel." He didn't look out from under his arm.

"So, stop weaseling and answer the question."

With each second that he lay there in silence, Mallory could feel herself growing colder despite the warm evening.

"I can't."

Mallory rocked back. She'd shared so much with him. Had been fearing the end of the summer, of this fire. She'd never given herself to someone so completely—never! The sex, the holding, the caring—they had become a little bubble of cosmic perfection until the moment Tyrone-Barlow-whoever-the-hell-he-was had busted it all apart.

She scrabbled around in the dark for her pants and boots. To hell with her underwear, wherever it had gone.

"Mallory?"

No way she was going to answer him.

"Can you help me?"

"Help you?" She spoke despite herself. "Think up another fake name so you can lie to me some more?"

"No," his voice sounded so sad that she stopped with one boot on and one boot off. He'd even tied her bootlaces for her. She stuffed the laces into her boot top rather than try to figure it out in the dark.

"Then what?"

"I have to tell Curt and Jana the truth. But I don't know how to do it."

"The truth is easy. You just say it." Which wasn't the truth at all. Her parents kept pushing her away because of her own truth. "Okay. That's wrong. It can be hard as hell, but you say it anyway."

Ty lay still. He didn't argue, and she didn't quite have the heart to leave him there.

14

Ty tried to get Jana and Curt off alone. But it
didn't work.

The Firebirds had been released overnight. It was just
past dawn and they were loading up the helos on the
trailers, doublechecking that they had all their gear, and
saying their goodbyes. Two other outfits were released as
well—the rest were still in full firefight hustle. The wide
pavement in front of the Zulies' headquarters were a mass
of people and machinery.

He and Mallory had spread out their sleeping bags
separately. Not far apart, but apart. And he'd missed her
every minute of the sleepless night as he'd watched the
slowly turning stars.

But he finally got Jana and Curt aside, sitting on one of
the lowboy trailers while he stood awkwardly in front of
them not knowing where to begin.

Before he could, Jasper and Stacy naturally gravitated
over and sat with their partners.

And wherever the other two women went, Maggie
joined. Of course she was holding hands with Palo. Then

it was clear that Drew and Amos didn't want to be left out of whatever was happening. Soon they were all crowded around, some on the edge of the lowboy, others in lawn chairs. Someone gave him one and he dropped into it. Mallory slipped elegantly into the one beside him—after moving it a slight distance away.

The truth, in his opinion, totally sucked.

He thought he'd blown it totally with Mallory last night, but she was still here. Maybe there was a sliver of hope. It was all he had, so he'd use that.

"I'm done for the season."

No surprise there. The long fire had burned to within two days of his already announced departure date.

"Missoula's my home town. I grew up here. I go—" another piece of the lie. "I went to college here."

Only Mallory glanced at him at that admission.

"I…" It caught in his throat.

The truth *was* hard to say.

"I'm not—" He balled his fists to fight the tears as his throat choked off.

"He's not Ty Franks," Mallory said for him softly. He didn't know whether to be angry for her unfairly taking the load that was his shit or hug her in thanks. Except he'd given up that privilege—all because of the goddamn lie in the first place. But still, she'd helped cover for him, just as he'd helped when Mallory had fixated on Jana's hooks after the hospital.

The head of the New Mexico hotshot team came over to say goodbye before they loaded up for the long drive to a Santa Rosa fire in Northern Cal.

Once he left, Ty forced himself to look around the circle of these people he'd come to know so well over the summer.

Mostly puzzled. Pissed would come soon enough.

Except Jana. She was smiling at him. Except Jana never smiled.

"I was wondering how long you were going to sit on that," her smile didn't abate.

He opened his mouth, but no sound came out.

"I pay you every two weeks, Ty. I also report it to the government. They contacted me about a name discrepancy for the Social Security number that you gave me."

"A…"

"What's going on?" Curt turned to his sister.

"Ty's real name is Barlow Williams." Now Jana was the one speaking for him.

"That's weird. Same as Dad?"

"The Second," Jana finished.

"That really weird," Curt continued to look confused.

Stacy held Curt's hand more tightly and blinked in surprise a couple of times then gave a puzzled laugh, "I have a brother-in-law?"

"You have a what?" Curt looked at his wife.

"Half-brother-in-law," Jana corrected.

Ty was trying desperately to get a handle on what was happening. They were supposed to be angry or… or something! He turned to Mallory, but she was keeping her lovely face carefully blank.

"So he's…" Curt stopped himself. "So we're…" he waved a finger back and forth between his own chest and Ty's. "That's beyond really weird."

"Weird wasn't my word for it," Ty was surprised he could speak.

"Pissed as hell," Jasper said quietly from under the brim of his cowboy hat. "How did you find out?"

"I found your dad's, *our* dad's name on the marriage license while going through Mom's shit after she died last year. I searched online and you guys popped up. She told me my dad had died when I was a little boy. In a car accident. Even though I found notes of meetings in hotels, and a vacation together when I was fifteen. I don't think I ever met him. Not once."

"Marriage license? Dad married both your mom *and* ours?" Curt shook his head but couldn't seem to clear it. "What's worse than beyond weird?"

"Mega-weird?" Mallory suggested and Curt nodded his agreement.

"Car wreck came true twenty years later," Jana stayed her usual totally chill, rational self. "I wonder if he lived long enough after the accident to see the irony."

Then she looked right at him.

"Our mom was pretty good. Dad was always a self-centered prick."

"Hey!" Curt protested.

"He was, Curt," Jana said with a sigh before turning back to Ty. "Your half-brother always thinks the best of people. Kind of a blind spot."

Ty knew that. Couldn't miss it because that *was* the kind of guy Curt was. None of this was going the way he expected. He glanced over at Mallory who was watching him carefully.

Truth is as hard as hell, but you say it anyway.

He knew that if he wanted even a half chance with her, he'd have to come clean, all the way.

She nodded once, as if she could read what he was thinking.

He reached out his hand and, after a moment's hesitation, she took it. It was the strongest he ever felt. He turned back to his unknown family, knowing what he had to do.

"I'm broke. I can't pay for college. Mom died busted

too. Jasper's right, I was so furious when I found out you two had your pretty little Firebirds. I—" This was worse than hard.

Mallory squeezed his hand, so he closed his eyes and blurted it out.

"I came here to screw you guys. Gather information, get some dirt on you. Sue you for half of the money. He was my dad, too." Despite the bigamy and lies and never wanting to see him and— Remembering his mom's strength at the end was all that let him keep it together.

"Does it make you feel any better to know that after we sold the house and everything else, we ended up *owing* over twenty thousand dollars?"

"Why was that anyway?" Curt asked.

"You remember how money slid through his fingers. Cars, the boat. The helicopter lessons that he paid for without even blinking… All of it. Remember how many times he changed jobs yet we were always broke? The fights he and Mom always had about money?" Jana waved her hooks in the air like she was brushing it away.

Curt grunted as she jogged his memory.

Ty had always thought they were so lucky because they got to have their father and he didn't. But Ty and his mom had never fought. Money had been tight, but they'd both been careful and worked hard. She insisted that college was his way out, but that hadn't come together and he hadn't had the heart to tell her about what a waste it all was—even with in-state tuition and scholarships covering most of it.

He and Mom had been a team. Them against the world. It sounds like Barlow the First maybe hadn't been such a great gift after all.

But Ty couldn't help looking at the six glistening helicopters perched on their trailers behind the three black pickups. He'd looked it up and the six helos cost over ten million dollars.

"Army disability pay. Gave me a medal and bump in rank on my way out the door for this," Jana held up her prosthetic hand. "Also every penny Curt and Jasper had set aside in six years of flying to fire. We started the season hocked out to everybody. We've paid off the trucks and one of the helicopters, better than I thought. Might own a second by end of season. The rest are a lease and a prayer."

Ty started to laugh. He couldn't help it.

Jana waited him out. Somehow his half-sister was the only one to get the joke. No, Mallory's smile said that she did too.

"Well, that was another one of my famous plans gone bust."

The others started laughing too, but Jana stayed serious until the others quieted.

She leaned in and really looked him in the eye.

"The Ty that first showed up to join us, I'm guessing that's not the kind of person your mother raised."

And with those simple words, Ty felt more like crying than laughing.

"You've been with us all summer. You've done a great job. So, I'm going to make you an offer."

He could only blink in surprise.

"You've mentioned college only three times all summer. I'm guessing it doesn't have you hooked."

Ty looked up at her, "Kind of obvious, huh?"

"Been watching you with Maggie. She says you've got good instincts about aircraft."

"You've talked about me…" He shut his mouth.

"How about the Firebirds fund you for an airframe-

and-powerplant course. To pay it off, you come back as assistant mechanic next spring?"

"You'd do that?" Ty tried to gauge his own reaction, but couldn't get a handle on it. It was too big to make sense of all at once.

Jana nodded.

"Why?" Still unable to measure it, he thought how it had felt to help rebuild those engines. It had been fascinating how they actually worked. He could still see it in his head.

"It's not because we're related to the same selfish prick. It's because you're good people. You spent a whole summer proving that despite yourself, Ty. Think about that. You might also want to think about changing at least your first name. Ty fits you way better than some jerk named Barlow. And if I needed more proof that you're good people…" she nodded at Mallory.

It was hard, but Ty made himself look over at her. What was her reaction to all this?

Somehow, impossibly, Mallory looked at him like she believed in him.

"But…" —if he was with the Firebirds and she was a smokie for Mount Hood, they'd never be together. And that suddenly struck him as the very worst thing that could ever happen.

"One more season with us. I called Denise with MHA. She said she'd look you over after a second season under Maggie's thumb. If you're as good as Maggie and I think you can be, you could go wrench for Mallory's outfit. By the way, there's a top A&P mechanic's course about ten miles from where Mallory and her busted wrist will be stuck in a classroom all winter studying forestry."

Jana rose to her feet and Ty could only stumble to his.

Because Mallory hadn't let go of his hand, she rose with him—and took a half step closer.

"We're going down to the passenger terminal and get a decent breakfast before we hit the road. If you two decide you want a lift back to Portland, we could probably make some space."

And the Firebirds all headed after Jana.

Maggie gave him a thumbs up. Stacy left behind a quick hug. Amos and Drew stopped just long enough to tell Mallory that she was too pretty for him and should consider a real man.

Curt shook his hand, strong and solid. "Still say it's beyond mega-weird."

Jasper just nodded from beneath his cowboy hat the way he always did.

Then there was just the two of them standing beside the big pickups. With his free hand, he reached out to stroke his fingers over one of the MD 520Ns. They were so beautiful. Brilliant machines that did a tough job in a very special way.

Even though he could feel her hand still in his, it was difficult to turn and look at Mallory. When he finally did, the sun caught her hair and blazed brilliantly.

"Mallory?" Ty didn't know what the question was, and by her bright blush, neither did she.

"You—" she gasped a little, then caught her breath. He saw the smokejumper come over her as she stood straighter and looked him square in the eye. "You did that great. And you see the real me. Do you have any idea what a gift that is?"

"Yeah. No one sees me." He'd spent a whole life being an outsider to everyone except his mom.

Mallory took that final half step to him and rested a hand on his cheek, "I do."

"And you want to be around me, despite that?"

She didn't answer him with a smile, she used a kiss instead.

He wrapped his arms around her and buried his face in her glorious hair. He'd been keeping his distance for far too long.

There was a new truth and they both held it close because it was the best thing they'd ever do.

WILDFIRE AT DAWN (EXCERPT)

IF YOU LIKED THIS, YOU'LL LOVE THE
SMOKEJUMPER NOVELS!

WILDFIRE AT DAWN

(EXCERPT)

$\mathcal{M}$ount Hood Aviation's lead smokejumper Johnny Akbar Jepps rolled out of his lower bunk careful not to bang his head on the upper. Well, he tried to roll out, but every muscle fought him, making it more a crawl than a roll. He checked the clock on his phone. Late morning.

He'd slept twenty of the last twenty-four hours and his body felt as if he'd spent the entire time in one position. The coarse plank flooring had been worn smooth by thousands of feet hitting exactly this same spot year in and year out for decades. He managed to stand upright…then he felt it, his shoulders and legs screamed.

Oh, right.

The New Tillamook Burn. Just about the nastiest damn blaze he'd fought in a decade of jumping wildfires. Two hundred thousand acres—over three hundred square miles—of rugged Pacific Coast Range forest, poof! The worst forest fire in a decade for the Pacific Northwest, but they'd killed it off without a single fatality or losing a single town. There'd been a few bigger ones, out in the flatter eastern part of Oregon state. But that much area—mostly on terrain too steep to climb even when it wasn't on fire—had been a horror.

Akbar opened the blackout curtain and winced against the summer brightness of blue sky and towering trees that lined the firefighter's camp. Tim was gone from the upper bunk, without kicking Akbar on his way out. He must have been as hazed out as Akbar felt.

He did a couple of side stretches and could feel every single minute of the eight straight days on the wildfire to contain the bastard, then the excruciating nine days more to convince it that it was dead enough to hand off to a Type II incident mop-up crew. Not since his beginning days on a hotshot crew had he spent seventeen days on a single fire.

And in all that time nothing more than catnaps in the acrid safety of the "black"—the burned-over section of a fire, black with char and stark with no hint of green foliage. The mop-up crews would be out there for weeks before it was dead past restarting, but at least it was truly done in. That fire wasn't merely contained; they'd killed it bad.

Yesterday morning, after demobilizing, his team of smokies had pitched into their bunks. No wonder he was so damned sore. His stretches worked out the worst of the kinks but he still must be looking like an old man stumbling about.

He looked down at the sheets. Damn it. They'd been fresh before he went to the fire, now he'd have to wash them again. He'd been too exhausted to shower before sleeping and they were all smeared with the dirt and soot that he could still feel caking his skin. Two-Tall Tim, his number two man and as tall as two of Akbar, kinda, wasn't in his bunk. His towel was missing from the hook.

Shower. Shower would be good. He grabbed his own

towel and headed down the dark, narrow hall to the far end of the bunk house. Every one of the dozen doors of his smoke teams were still closed, smokies still sacked out. A glance down another corridor and he could see that at least a couple of the Mount Hood Aviation helicopter crews were up, but most still had closed doors with no hint of light from open curtains sliding under them. All of MHA had gone above and beyond on this one.

"Hey, Tim." Sure enough, the tall Eurasian was in one of the shower stalls, propped up against the back wall letting the hot water stream over him.

"Akbar the Great lives," Two-Tall sounded half asleep.

"Mostly. Doghouse?" Akbar stripped down and hit the next stall. The old plywood dividers were flimsy with age and gray with too many showers. The Mount Hood Aviation firefighters' Hoodie One base camp had been a kids' summer camp for decades. Long since defunct, MHA had taken it over and converted the playfields into landing areas for their helicopters, and regraded the main road into a decent airstrip for the spotter and jump planes.

"Doghouse? Hell, yeah. I'm like ten thousand calories short." Two-Tall found some energy in his voice at the idea of a trip into town.

The Doghouse Inn was in the nearest town. Hood River lay about a half hour down the mountain and had exactly what they needed: smokejumper-sized portions and a very high ratio of awesomely fit young women come to windsurf the Columbia Gorge. The Gorge, which formed the Washington and Oregon border, provided a fantastically target-rich environment for a smokejumper too long in the woods.

"You're too tall to be short of anything," Akbar knew he was being a little slow to reply, but he'd only been awake for minutes.

"You're like a hundred thousand calories short of being even a halfway decent size," Tim was obviously recovering faster than he was.

"Just because my parents loved me instead of tying me to a rack every night ain't my problem, buddy."

He scrubbed and soaped and scrubbed some more until he felt mostly clean.

"I'm telling you, Two-Tall. Whoever invented the hot shower, that's the dude we should give the Nobel prize to."

"You say that every time."

"You arguing?"

He heard Tim give a satisfied groan as some muscle finally let go under the steamy hot water. "Not for a second."

Akbar stepped out and walked over to the line of sinks, smearing a hand back and forth to wipe the condensation from the sheet of stainless steel screwed to the wall. His hazy reflection still sported several smears of char.

"You so purdy, Akbar."

"Purdier than you, Two-Tall." He headed back into the shower to get the last of it.

"So not. You're jealous."

Akbar wasn't the least bit jealous. Yes, despite his lean height, Tim was handsome enough to sweep up any ladies he wanted.

But on his own, Akbar did pretty damn well himself. What he didn't have in height, he made up for with a proper smokejumper's muscled build. Mixed with his tan-dark Indian complexion, he did fine.

The real fun, of course, was when the two of them went cruising together. The women never knew what to make of the two of them side by side. The contrast kept them off balance enough to open even more doors.

He smiled as he toweled down. It also didn't hurt that

their opening answer to "what do you do" was "I jump out of planes to fight forest fires."

Worked every damn time. God he loved this job.

THE SMALL TOWN of Hood River, a winding half-an-hour down the mountain from the MHA base camp, was hopping. Mid-June, colleges letting out. Students and the younger set of professors high-tailing it to the Gorge. They packed the bars and breweries and sidewalk cafes. Suddenly every other car on the street had a windsurfing board tied on the roof.

The snooty rich folks were up at the historic Timberline Lodge on Mount Hood itself, not far in the other direction from MHA. Down here it was a younger, thrill seeker set and you could feel the energy.

There were other restaurants in town that might have better pickings, but the Doghouse Inn was MHA tradition and it was a good luck charm—no smokie in his right mind messed with that. This was the bar where all of the MHA crew hung out. It didn't look like much from the outside, just a worn old brick building beaten by the Gorge's violent weather. Aged before its time, which had been long ago.

But inside was awesome. A long wooden bar stretched down one side with a half-jillion microbrew taps and a small but well-stocked kitchen at the far end. The dark wood paneling, even on the ceiling, was barely visible beneath thousands of pictures of doghouses sent from patrons all over the world. Miniature dachshunds in ornately decorated shoeboxes, massive Newfoundlands in backyard mansions that could easily house hundreds of their smaller kin, and everything in between. A gigantic

Snoopy atop his doghouse in full Red Baron fighting gear dominated the far wall. Rumor said Shulz himself had been here two owners before and drawn it.

Tables were grouped close together, some for standing and drinking, others for sitting and eating.

"Amy, sweetheart!" Two-Tall called out as they entered the bar. The perky redhead came out from behind the bar to receive a hug from Tim. Akbar got one in turn, so he wasn't complaining. Cute as could be and about his height; her hugs were better than taking most women to bed. Of course, Gerald the cook and the bar's co-owner was big enough and strong enough to squish either Tim or Akbar if they got even a tiny step out of line with his wife. Gerald was one amazingly lucky man.

Akbar grabbed a Walking Man stout and turned to assess the crowd. A couple of the air jocks were in. Carly and Steve were at a little table for two in the corner, obviously not interested in anyone's company but each others. Damn, that had happened fast. New guy on the base swept up one of the most beautiful women on the planet. One of these days he'd have to ask Steve how he'd done that. Or maybe not. It looked like they were settling in for the long haul; the big "M" was so not his own first choice.

Carly was also one of the best FBANs in the business. Akbar was a good Fire Behavior Analyst, had to be or he wouldn't have made it to first stick—lead smokie of the whole MHA crew. But Carly was something else again. He'd always found the Flame Witch, as she was often called, daunting and a bit scary besides; she knew the fire better than it did itself. Steve had latched on to one seriously driven lady. More power to him.

The selection of female tourists was especially good today, but no other smokies in yet. They'd be in soon enough…most of them had groaned awake and said they were coming as he and Two-Tall kicked their hallway doors, but not until they'd been on their way out—he and Tim had first pick. Actually some of the smokies were coming, others had told them quite succinctly where they could go—but hey, jumping into fiery hell is what they did for a living anyway, so no big change there.

A couple of the chopper pilots had nailed down a big table right in the middle of the bustling seating area: Jeannie, Mickey, and Vern. Good "field of fire" in the immediate area.

He and Tim headed over, but Akbar managed to snag the chair closest to the really hot lady with down-her-back curling dark-auburn hair at the next table over—set just right to see her profile easily. Hard shot, sitting there with her parents, but damn she was amazing. And if that was her mom, it said the woman would be good looking for a long time to come.

Two-Tall grimaced at him and Akbar offered him a comfortable "beat out your ass" grin. But this one didn't feel like that. Maybe it was the whole parental thing. He sat back and kept his mouth shut.

He made sure that Two-Tall could see his interest. That made Tim honor bound to try and cut Akbar out of the running.

LAURA JENSON HAD SPOTTED them coming into the restaurant. Her dad was only moments behind.

"Those two are walking like they just climbed off their first-ever horseback ride."

She had to laugh, they did. So stiff and awkward they barely managed to move upright. They didn't look like first-time windsurfers, aching from the unexpected workout. They'd also walked in like they thought they were two gifts to god, which was even funnier. She turned away to avoid laughing in their faces. Guys who thought like that rarely appreciated getting a reality check.

Available at fine retailers everywhere.

ABOUT THE AUTHOR

M.L. Buchman started the first of, what is now over 50 novels and as many short stories, while flying from South Korea to ride his bicycle across the Australian Outback. Part of a solo around-the-world trip that ultimately launched his writing career.

All three of his military romantic suspense series—The Night Stalkers, Firehawks, and Delta Force—have had a title named "Top 10 Romance of the Year" by the American Library Association's *Booklist*. He also writes: contemporary romance, thrillers, and fantasy.

Past lives include: years as a project manager, rebuilding and single-handing a fifty-foot sailboat, both flying and jumping out of airplanes, and he has designed and built two houses. He is now making his living as a full-time writer on the Oregon Coast with his beloved wife and is constantly amazed at what you can do with a degree in Geophysics. You may keep up with his writing and receive a free book by subscribing to his newsletter at: www.mlbuchman.com

Join the conversation:
www.mlbuchman.com

Other works by M. L. Buchman:

www.ingramcontent.com/pod-product-compliance
Lightning Source LLC
Chambersburg PA
CBHW051712180726
48283CB00004B/1320